Circus animals have come to town!

The hungry hippo
is just waking up.

A pretty performer
holds a hoop for a pup.

The mighty elephants
can stand up tall,

And playful seals
toss a bright ball.

A bear on a bike —
what a sight!

We hope the lion
won't take a bite!